ON THE ROAD

with Mavis and Marge

For
Aoibhe

First published 2010 by Walker Books Ltd

87 Vauxhall Walk, London SE11 5HJ

This edition published 2011

10 9 8 7 6 5 4 3 2

© 2010 Niamh Sharkey

This book has been typeset in Kingthings Trypewriter

Printed in China

British Library Cataloguing in Publication Data:
a catalogue record for this book is available
from the British Library

ISBN 978-1-4063-2998-8

www.niamhsharkey.com

www.walker.co.uk

ON THE ROAD

with Mavis and Marge

NIAMH SHARKEY

WALKER BOOKS
AND SUBSIDIARIES
LONDON · BOSTON · SYDNEY · AUCKLAND

Mavis was different to other cows. She was hungry for adventure.

Marge was smarter than your average chicken. She wanted to go where no chicken had gone before.

They knew there was a world out there waiting to be explored.

So they took the bike from the barn, said goodbye to their friends and off they went.

The bike got
a puncture.

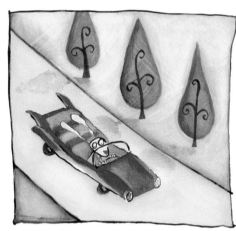

So what
luck to meet
Clarence, out
for a spin
in his car.

Uphill ...

downhill ...

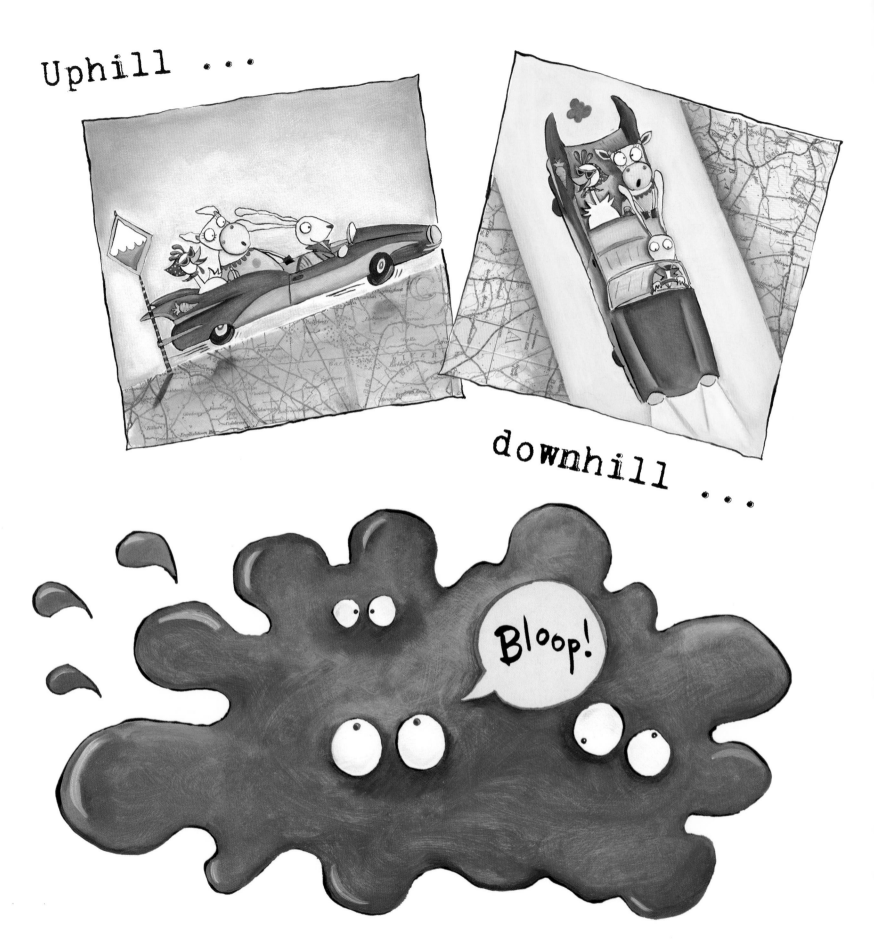

through puddles they drove.

Over bridges ...

through the forest ...

all the way to the ocean.

What luck! They landed
in Benny's boat!

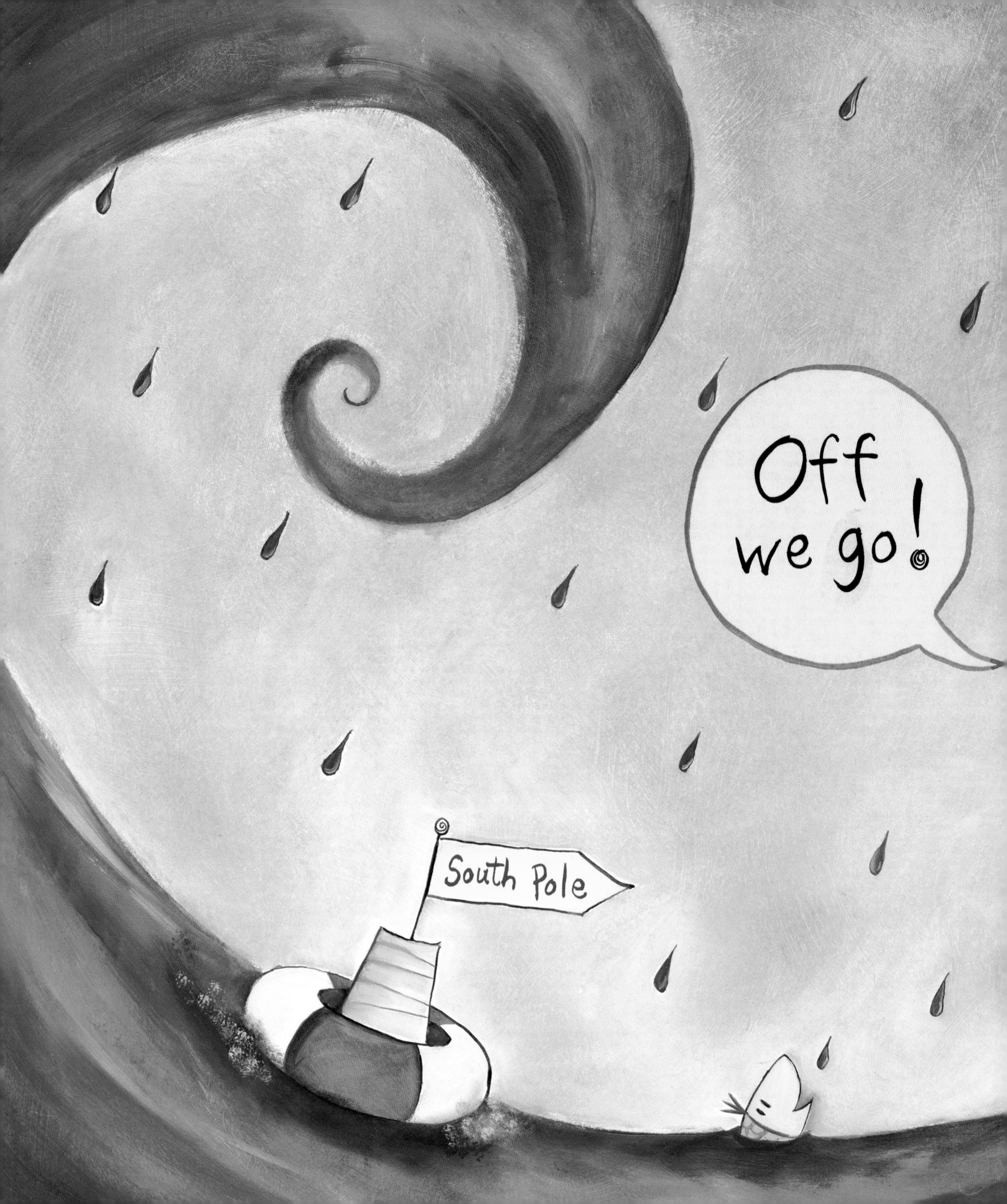
Off we go!
South Pole

Oh no!
BANG!

They hit an iceberg!

South Pole

Oh... we're lost.

What luck to bump into Albert.

I know the way!

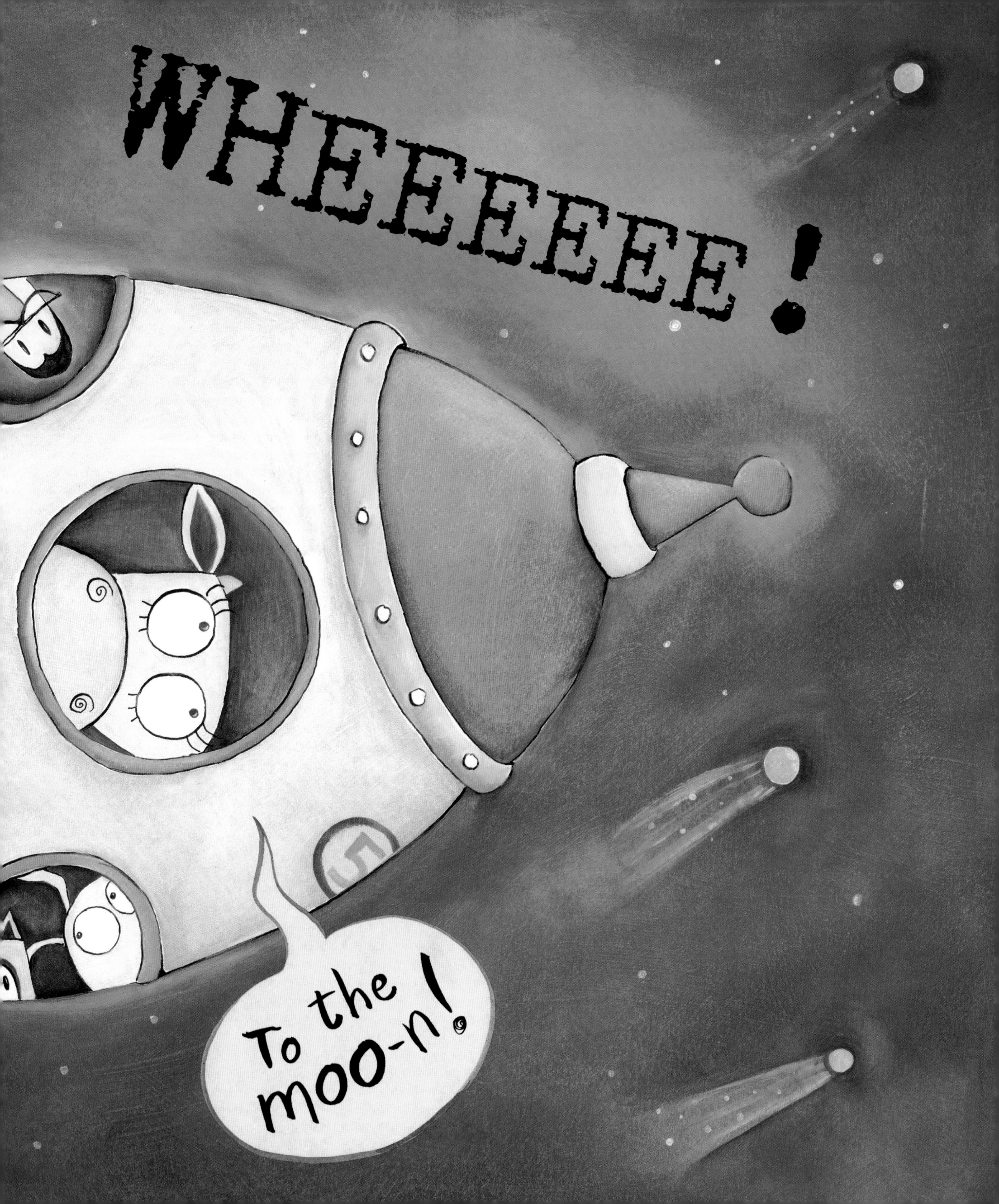
WHEEEEEE!
To the moo-n!

Mavis and Marge,
Clarence, Benny and
Albert all loved it
on the moon.

But then...

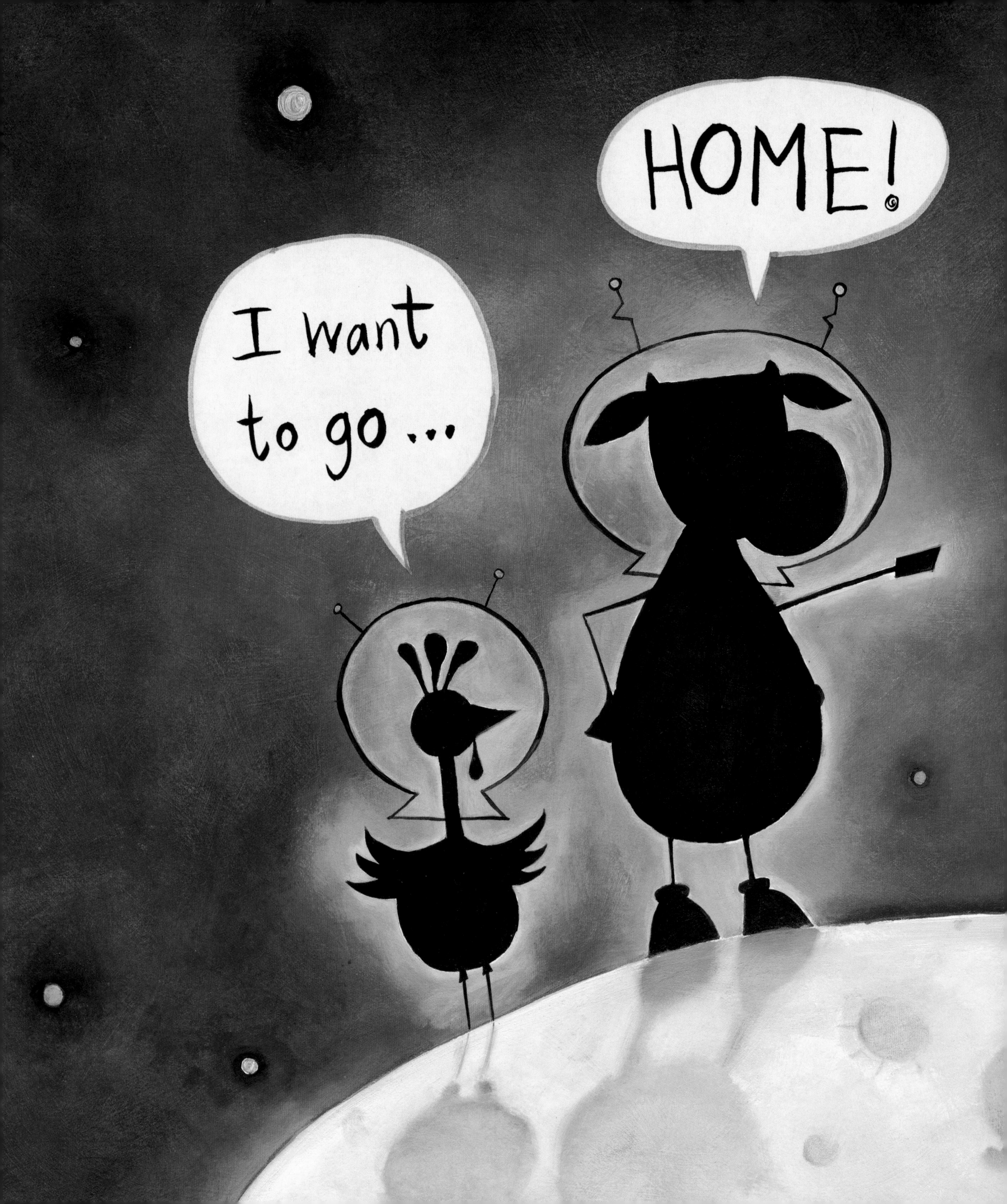
I want to go...
HOME!

So they
all went
home.

WHEEEEEE!

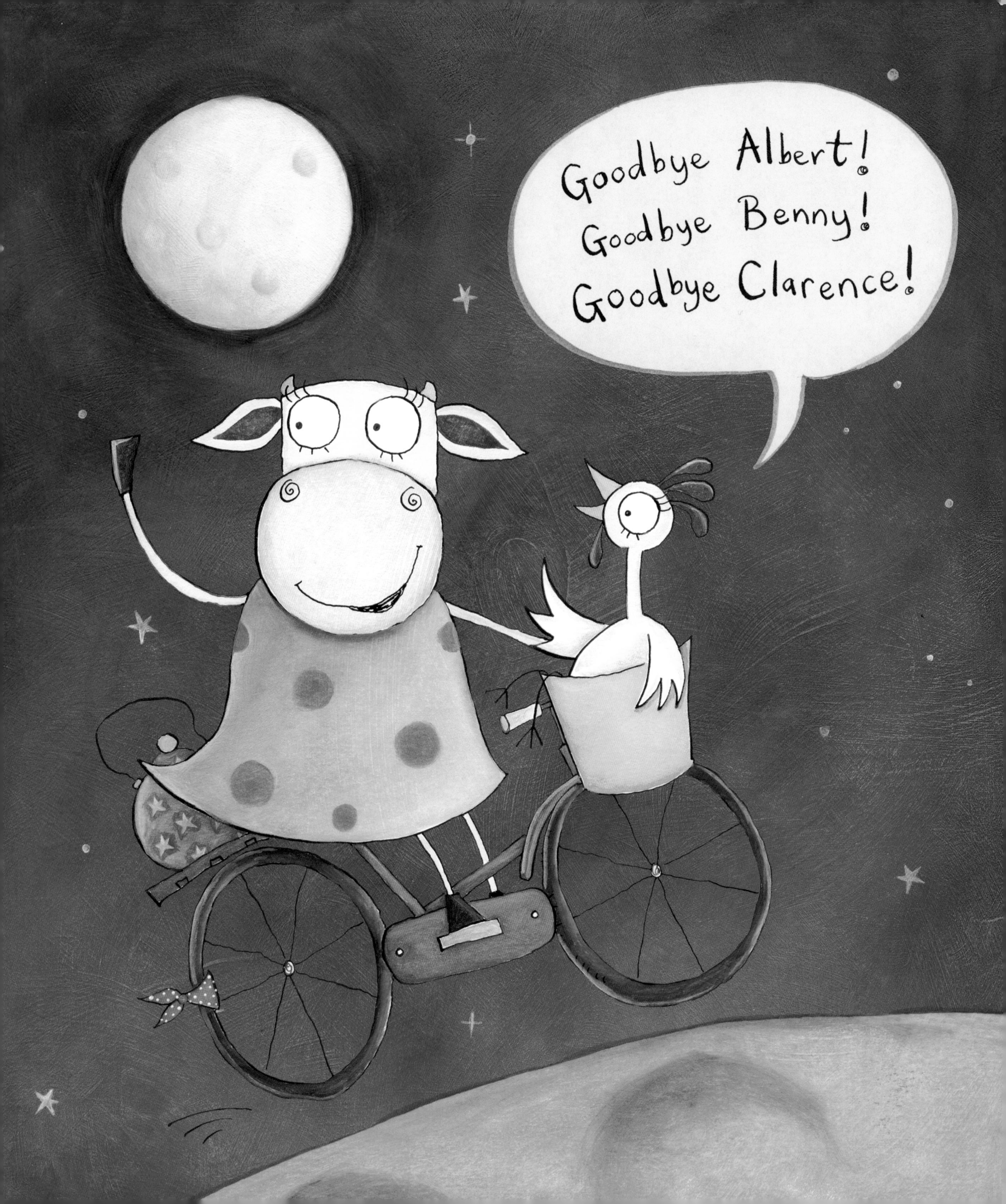
Goodbye Albert!
Goodbye Benny!
Goodbye Clarence!

Life on the road had been a great adventure, but Mavis and Marge agreed...